For all the summer reading clubs
—C. R.

For Cynthia Rylant, with thanks and admiration
—S. S.

SIMON SPOTLIGHT
An imprint of Simon & Schuster Children's Publishing Division
1230 Avenue of the Americas, New York, NY 10020
Text copyright © 2011 by Cynthia Rylant
Illustrations copyright © 2011 by Suçie Stevenson
All rights reserved, including the right of reproduction in whole or in part in any form.
SIMON SPOTLIGHT, READY-TO-READ, and colophon are
registered trademarks of Simon & Schuster, Inc.
For information about special discounts for bulk purchases, please contact
Simon & Schuster Special Sales at 1-866-506-1949 or business@simonandschuster.com.
The Simon & Schuster Speakers Bureau can bring authors to your live event. For more
information or to book an event contact the Simon & Schuster Speakers Bureau
at 1-866-248-3049 or visit our website at www.simonspeakers.com.
Designed by Tom Daly
The text of this book was set in Goudy Old Style.
The illustrations for this book were rendered in pen-and-ink and watercolor.
Manufactured in China 1110 SCP
First Simon Spotlight hardcover edition February 2011
2 4 6 8 10 9 7 5 3 1
Library of Congress Cataloging-in-Publication Data
Rylant, Cynthia.
Annie and Snowball and the Book Bugs Club :
the ninth book of their adventures / by Cynthia Rylant ;
illustrated by Suçie Stevenson. — 1st ed.
p. cm. — (Ready-to-read)
Summary: Annie and Henry join the summer reading club
at the library, and vow to be "Book Bugs" for life.
ISBN 978-1-4169-7199-3 (hardcover)
[1. Books and reading—Fiction. 2. Clubs—Fiction.
3. Summer—Fiction.] I. Stevenson, Suçie, ill. II. Title.
PZ7.R982Anb 2011
[E]—dc22
2009054125

Annie and Snowball and the Book Bugs Club

The Ninth Book of Their Adventures

Cynthia Rylant

Illustrated by Suçie Stevenson

READY-TO-READ

SIMON SPOTLIGHT

New York   London   Toronto   Sydney

Contents

Summer!

Summer was here and
Annie was having a wonderful time.
She was riding bikes
with cousin Henry
and his big dog, Mudge.

She was swimming at the local pool.

She was tending a lettuce garden
for her bunny, Snowball.

Annie was having so much fun!
And more fun was just around the corner.

In fact it was around the corner
at the library.

8

The library had a sign out front that said:
JOIN THE BOOK BUGS CLUB.

"What's a book bug?" Annie asked Henry.

"I think it's a book club," said Henry.

"A book club?" said Annie.

She was so excited.

Annie had always wanted
to be in a book club.
"Let's join!" said Annie.

"Hmm," said Henry.
He needed to think about it.

In the summer Henry liked to do
things with Mudge.
Outside things.

Running, rolling, riding things.

A book club was not a
running, rolling, riding thing.

But Henry could tell that
Annie really wanted to join.

And Annie always did things
Henry liked to do.

14

She was great at Frisbee
and tree climbing.

15

Henry decided it was time
to do an Annie-thing.
"Okay!" Henry said. "Let's join!"
Mudge waited outside by the two lions
while Annie and Henry went in.

Mr. Malk

The librarian was really nice
to Annie and Henry.
His name was Mr. Malk,
and he was wearing
a great tie with cats on it.

He welcomed Annie and Henry
to the Book Bugs Club.

He gave them special pencils and
special notebooks.

He told them to read and read and read.
And to put in their notebooks
the titles of the books they read.

He said they would get
stickers and stars and other fun things
for the books they read.

He said there would be book picnics.
"Cool!" said Henry.
Henry was happy to hear that.

Picnics were outside things
that Mudge could attend.

Mr. Malk invited Annie and Henry
to check out books to read.

And they did!
When they left the library,
they each had a big pile of books.

Mudge sniffed and sniffed the books.

"Nothing to eat, Mudge," said Annie.

Mudge wagged.

He was happy to see them anyway.

Reading!

Annie and Snowball and
Henry and Mudge
found many good
summer reading places.

They read on the backyard swing.

They read on the front porch steps.

They read under the maple tree.

They read in the maple tree.

(Well, two of them read there.)

It looked like a book club
was an outside thing as well
as an inside thing!
Annie and Henry read and read.

Henry was reading all the adventures
of a mouse pirate.
There were many books
about the mouse pirate,
and Henry was going to read them all.

Annie was reading every fairy tale
she could find.
She didn't know there were
so many fairy tales!

30

They took their notebooks to the library,
and Mr. Malk gave them
stars and stickers
for all the books they read.

And the best was yet to come:
a Book Bugs picnic!

Book Bugs Forever

On the day of the picnic,
all of the Book Bugs in town
went to the park.
Annie and Snowball and
Henry and Mudge went too.

33

There were a lot of Book Bugs!
"I didn't know there were
this many of us," Henry said to Annie.
The Book Bugs were all given special
hats to wear.
Even Snowball and Mudge.

And they played book ball, book tag,
and book hide-and-seek.
It was so much fun!

Annie met a girl who had read
all the fairy tales too.
A new friend!

36

When the picnic was over,
everyone said thank you to Mr. Malk
for such a nice time.
Mudge gave him a drooly kiss.

Annie and Henry promised
to keep reading.
"We will be Book Bugs for life!"
they promised.

Mr. Malk was so happy to hear this
that he let Mudge have all of the
leftover hot dogs!
It was a wonderful day.